Rat

Rat

Lesley Choyce

orca soundings

ORCA BOOK PUBLISHERS

Library and Archives Canada Cataloguing in Publication

Choyce, Lesley
Rat / Lesley Choyce
(Orca soundings)

Issued also in electronic formats.
ISBN 978-1-4598-0301-5 (bound).--ISBN 978-1-4598-0300-8 (pbk.)

I. Title. II. Series: Orca soundings.
PS8555.H668R38 2012   jC813'.54   C2012-902573-9

First published in the United States, 2012
Library of Congress Control Number: 2012938207

Summary: Tired of bullies at school, Colin decides to take a stand. Branded
a rat, he finds that standing up for what you believe in can be empowering.

MIX
Paper from
responsible sources
FSC® C016245
www.fsc.org

*Orca Book Publishers is dedicated to preserving the environment and has printed
this book on paper certified by the Forest Stewardship Council®.*

Orca Book Publishers gratefully acknowledges the support for its publishing
programs provided by the following agencies: the Government of Canada
through the Canada Book Fund and the Canada Council for the Arts,
and the Province of British Columbia through the BC Arts Council
and the Book Publishing Tax Credit.

Cover photography by Dreamstime.com

ORCA BOOK PUBLISHERS
PO Box 5626, Stn. B
Victoria, BC Canada
v8R 6s4

ORCA BOOK PUBLISHERS
PO Box 468
Custer, WA USA
98240-0468

www.orcabook.com
Printed and bound in Canada.

15 14 13 12 • 4 3 2 1

Chapter One

It's not like I've assigned myself the job of protector of the weak or anything. I just get tired of creeps at school harassing people who don't deserve it. I mean, a lot of things really piss me off. School in general pisses me off. And that includes the teachers. Most of them see me as a troublemaker, and I wouldn't want to have it any other way.

But there are some kids at school who are hard at work practicing to be the true scum of the earth. You know the type I'm talking about. If you're not the one being worked over in one way or another by these dorks, then you just turn the other way. We all know the drill. Don't get involved. Don't rat on anyone.

I just don't think it should work that way. Funny thing is, though, whenever I try to bring a little honesty into this crazy, screwed-up world, I'm the one who gets his ass kicked in one form or another.

Take this for example.

During lunchtime awhile back, I was walking back to school after eating a not-so-great greasy hamburger and stale French fries. I was reminding myself that my friend Emily was right. I should give up that crap and become a vegetarian. I was almost back to school and anxious to get on with what looked to be a monumentally boring afternoon. That's when

I saw Liam and Craig harassing some old geezer carrying a couple of bags of groceries. The old guy was kind of bent over and walking funny. I don't know why I even noticed. I was across the street, and there was a lot of traffic, but it was like I had radar or something.

So I crossed over right away, ignoring the cars honking at me and the one idiot who had to screech to a halt so he didn't kill me. He shot me the finger, and I thumped smartly on the hood of his Lexus.

I felt a knot in my stomach (it could have been the greasy burger) as I walked up to Liam and Craig. I heard Liam shouting at the old guy, "C'mon, I'm sure you have some spare cash you can lend us. You look like you have plenty." You had to be there to hear the real nastiness in the way he said this.

The old guy just shook his head and tried to keep walking. But just then,

Craig walked forward and put himself right in the way. The old man tried to walk around, but Craig had him covered again.

"Craig, you stupid piece of garbage," I shouted. "Leave him alone!"

Craig looked at me like I had punched him in the face.

"Leave him alone," I said again.

Liam gave me the once-over too, but then turned back to Mr. Groceries and said, "Maybe we can just make do with something in the bag. You got anything good in there?" Liam had his hand on the cloth grocery bag and was trying to reach inside. The old man was trying to pull away, and he mumbled something. That's when I realized that here was an old dude who was a little out of it and probably downright scared of these two grunge mongers. Craig was blocking the man's path, and Liam was still reaching into the bag. I'd had enough.

4

"Get out of his way," I yelled at Craig. And I grabbed Liam by the shoulder and was spinning him around. Liam looked shocked and angry.

"Colin," he said, "this has nothing to do with you. We're just having a little fun."

"Leave him alone," I insisted. The old man was moving away now as Liam and Craig stood toe-to-toe with me. I wasn't sure what would happen next. I knew I could outrun them if I had to. But that wouldn't matter. They'd get me one way or the other. So I just stood my ground.

I was about to launch into one of my lectures. It was always the wrong thing to do.

But then I heard the outside bell at school across the street. The end of lunch hour. Liam gave me a dirty look, and he put his index finger in the air in front of my face. That said it all. *This isn't over yet*. He tapped Craig on the shoulder, and they sprinted across the street toward school.

The old man was having a hard time. He was stumbling as he walked away and looked like he couldn't quite hold on to the bags he was carrying. He was very shaken up. So I ran toward him to see if I could help.

He half turned when he heard me coming. I slowed down and tried to explain that I wanted to help, but when I reached him, he dropped his bags and started screaming at me. He must have thought I was going to continue to harass him. Then he started smacking me. It didn't hurt, but it surprised me.

"Just get away," he screamed. "Leave me alone."

"I was trying to help," I said. But he kept yelling and hitting, so I backed off. Other people were looking at me. So I ran.

I was late for math class and feeling pretty crappy about it all, thinking my Good Samaritan days were definitely over. And that's when I was called down to Mr. Miller's office.

Chapter Two

Mr. Miller is the vice-principal. Our school is a big-city high school with big-city problems, and Miller had been brought in last year as a kind of troubleshooter. Word was that he'd wrestled knives from students and had faced down someone in his school with a gun.

Miller had a rep as being a hard-ass, and if you had a name as a troublemaker, he was on your case. That would be me. Not that I deserved it. I just had some problems with authority figures. School had a funny set of unwritten laws. It seemed to me that if you were sneaky about your dirty work and no teacher saw what you were up to, you could get away with a hell of a lot. Almost no one in the school was going to snitch on you. But if you were up front with your complaint or defiant in any public way, and honest about it, you found yourself called to the office and sitting across the desk from Mr. Miller.

Just like I was now.

"So, Colin, I'm sad to say your egregious behavior rather interrupted my lunch."

"I don't understand what *egregious* means." Just like Miller to use a big word like that.

"Egregious. As in shockingly bad."

"I don't understand," I said.

"You rarely do. But I was sitting here minding my own business, and I look out across the street and there you are getting bashed on by some little old man. What the hell did you do to him?"

So Miller saw that scene but not what came before. I let out an exasperated breath. "It was Liam and Craig harassing him, not me."

"I didn't see them anywhere. Just you. Best not to place the blame on someone else. It doesn't look good on you." Miller's eyes were drilling right through me. We'd had run-ins before. Mostly me giving arrogant teachers a hard time or refusing to do assignments that I thought were point-less and stupid.

I took a deep breath and explained what really happened. I was trying to keep my cool.

Miller wasn't buying any of it. "I just know what I saw."

"Appearances can be deceiving," I said.

"Indeed."

"And if you don't believe me," I said, "you'd be making an egregious error."

He smiled slightly. "At least your vocabulary is improving. But I'll be watching you."

Yeah, he would be watching. And he'd pass on the word to several of his favorite teachers. I didn't like this a bit. But I kept my mouth shut. The burger felt like lead in my gut as I headed back to math class.

I kept my head low for the rest of the day and got the hell out of school when the final bell rang. At home, I holed up in my room and read a book about living with gorillas in Africa. Ever since I was a kid, I had a thing about animals—all animals. I still read books about gorillas and tigers, crocodiles and meerkats. Someday I'll work with wild animals. I like them better than people. But there weren't many wild animals where I lived in the north end of the city. Just birds, maybe, and some mice and rats. I took out my latest sketchbook and began to draw images of the animals in my head. Sketching always made me feel better. They never looked much like the real animals. More like some crazy fantasy-world version of animals. Big eyes, exaggerated features. My creatures. My animals.

That night, my friend Emily called. Like me, she's not very popular because she's different. She's vegan, and for some reason people find vegans annoying—maybe it's because they don't eat cheese. And she dresses funny—layers of anything, as long as it doesn't have a designer label. And hair in dreads that she almost never washes. But I still call her a friend, and outcasts need to stick together in high school.

"You didn't really post a photo of yourself naked, did you?" she blurted out.

"What?" I asked.

"On GoofFace. There's a photo of you without clothes on and your name right under it. It looks like you posted it yourself. Tell me you didn't do this."

"I didn't do this. It's somebody trying to make me look like an idiot." I flipped my book closed and turned to my computer. I hated sites like GoofFace, where anyone could put up lies or pictures or…anything. I went to the site and keyed in my own name. Yep. There it was. "It's my face—from last year's yearbook, I'd say. But it's definitely not my body."

"Pretty good Photoshop job, then," Emily said.

"How many people do you think have seen this?" I asked.

There was a pause. "Well, I got a message from Marissa, and she picked it up from Twitter and…"

"So I guess just about everybody and anybody."

"Yep. Who would do this to you?"

It didn't take much brainpower to figure that one out. My current enemies, I was pretty sure, were tech savvy and fearless if they could do their dirty work anonymously.

I studied the photo again. Yep. My head attached to some other teenage boy's naked body. "Sucks to be me, I guess."

"Guess you could say that. Sorry, Colin. You don't deserve this. What are you going to do?"

"I don't know," I said, looking at the outrageous photo again. "But thanks for the heads-up. And, no, that is definitely not my body."

"Too bad," she said, trying to lighten things up. "I thought it was kind of cute—weird, but cute."

So I was up late that night trying to delete the image from the site, realizing it had probably already been copied and reposted god knows where around the world. We'd had a lecture on this stuff at school. The police had even said it was illegal to post such things. Right. Was I going to get blamed for this too?

It was getting really late, and I felt like I had to do something. So I rolled with it. I logged onto GoofFace and posted a comment on the fake photo. I wrote, *Although this is not a picture of my body, I'm thrilled to see someone took the time to do such a good job of manipulating the image. I can't say I'm opposed to nudity but question the motivation for such a creative effort.* And I left it at that. If I spoke my real thoughts, I figured I'd do more harm than good. Some things you just have to walk away from. Even if it's a fake image of what most people would believe was your own naked body.

I knew that Liam and Craig were your classic school bullies who now had new social-media tools and the Internet for their dirty work. Other kids like them had given me a pretty hard time when I was young. It hurt, and I dealt with it badly. But when I got older, something happened. I just stopped taking crap from people like them. I ended up in trouble more often than not. But it was worth it. And, for the most part, jerks like Liam and Craig gave up on me and chose other victims. There were always plenty of new victims. Now, though, with technology, it was easier than ever to nail someone to the cross.

As I tried to sleep, I couldn't help but try to come up with some kind of ultra-creative countermeasures to get back at the dorky duo. But I realized that the best revenge was to hold my head high and show the world I didn't give a rat's ass how many fake naked photos of me anyone posted on the Internet.

I wouldn't break that easily.

Chapter Three

Emily was waiting for me when I got to school. I figured half the kids at school had seen the photo. Almost everyone had opinions about me anyway. I was always doing something that got them talking. Protesting against final exams. Organizing a twenty-four-hour fast to end famine. Going to student council meetings and giving lectures to those geeks that they should stop wasting their time on the little things and take a stand and do something about something important. And now this.

"Do you know who did it?" Emily asked.

"Of course," I said confidently. "Yesterday I interrupted Craig and Liam when they were having fun."

"Ah," she said. "Cave Man and Lumpy. I should have guessed. You pissed them off, right? And now they see you as the enemy."

"You could say that. But I prefer to think of them as hostile friends." I liked Emily's nicknames for them. Yes, Craig looked a tad like he might have had Neanderthal parents, and Liam was, well, a bit on the lumpy side.

"You don't seem upset."

"What's to be upset about? It wasn't my body in those pics. People can believe what they want to believe. But I'm not an exhibitionist. How stupid is that? This isn't going to get to me. No big deal."

Emily got quiet.

"What?" I asked.

"You're not the only one targeted by Cave and Lump."

A lightbulb went on in my head. Maybe this wasn't just about me after all. "What do you mean?"

"Amanda. And Marissa. They had the same thing happen to them. They can't prove it, but they are pretty sure it's them. Craig was hitting on Amanda, and Liam had a thing for Marissa. When the boys got the cold shoulder—well, you can see how it works."

"You sure it was them?" I asked.

Emily nodded. "Pretty sure. But it's so easy to do this stuff anonymously these days. Anyone could do it."

"Those two turds should be flushed."

"Amanda's feeling so humiliated that she's been cutting school a lot.

You know what she's like," said Emily. "Marissa's trying to tough it out, but they both are getting some nasty postings, and some of the other guys think it's really them putting up their own pics. As you can imagine, they're taking some serious flak."

In English class, I didn't pay much attention to the teacher talking about poetry, but I kept thinking about the workings of a big high school like this. Classes are one thing, but in the halls, in the caf, in the bathrooms and everywhere else, things are happening. It's a circus, and half of what people think is real isn't. It's all about what you want to believe—who has done what, who is with whom, who is up and who is down. Everyone's trying to protect their own image, their own space. And you have people trying to tear you down whenever you look weak. Creeps trying to take advantage of you if you're a girl.

And if someone is a real jerk, you're not supposed to do anything about it—you're just supposed to walk away. Just thinking about it all got me pretty worked up.

I took a deep breath just as English was winding down. Mr. Winger was reading a poem by William Blake called "The Poison Tree." For some strange reason, it made sense to me. Anger and hate breeds more anger and hate. It actually made me think I needed a fresh approach to the current problem.

As soon as I left English, I went prowling for Cave and Lump. I noticed other kids in the hall looking at me. Some were laughing. Oh yeah. Big deal. But I couldn't find who I was looking for.

It wasn't until lunch that I caught up with them sitting by themselves near the windows eating gooey slabs of pizza. I sat down as if we were old friends. "Good work with the GoofFace thing,"

I told Liam. I was pretty sure it would have been his technical skills. He was a hard-core gamer and had picked up the skills. Craig was probably just along for the ride.

"Don't know what you're talking about," Liam said, biting down on a wad of pepperoni.

I smiled the most genuine grin I could muster. "Don't worry, dude. I'm good with it. All in fun, right?"

"Yeah," he said as Craig just kind of scrunched up his brow and didn't understand why I wasn't more pissed.

"Truth is, I found it rather flattering. I'm much skinnier than that guy's bod. But you're not doing this because you're gay, are you?"

Liam spit some of his pizza onto the paper plate and then looked me in the eye. "We could up the ante," Liam said. "You know that, don't you? We're still pretty disappointed in your intrusion yesterday."

23

"Hey, you can post whatever you want. I won't be offended."

Puzzlement again, this time on the part of both Cave and Lump.

"But I did take some flak yesterday from Miller," I added. "He thinks it was me roughing up the old guy."

"So you ratted on us instead, right?" Craig asked.

"What would have been the point?" I shot back. "He wouldn't believe anything I said. I'm not exactly on Miller's good list."

Craig gave me a smile. "Sweet," was all he said.

"But now that we've had this little talk," I continued, sounding a bit too much like a parody of myself, "I do have a favor to ask."

Both of them just stared at me like I was about to ask for a date with their mothers.

"Would you mind," I said as tact-fully as I could, "going easy on Amanda and Marissa?"

Liam's eyes widened a bit, and then he smiled at me and spoke in a tone that suggested we were friends, buddies, old allies who understood each other. "Colin, dude, hey, it's a way to get a girl to do what you want. I'm thinking that if I promise to take down those photos, one or the other might be willing to pay me back for my kindness."

I knew I wasn't about to change his mind on this. I gave him a small laugh—a fake one for sure, but he didn't know that. I said, "See you guys later," and I walked away.

Chapter Four

I half expected to get called into Miller's office over the photo thing, but that didn't happen. But what Liam had said was really bugging me. I arranged to meet Emily downtown at the Brown Bean Coffee House that night, and she showed up looking a bit tired and worried. I told her about my meeting with Cave and Lump. I tried to make the scene sound funny, but she wasn't taking it that way.

"I don't know, Colin. Things are just getting so creepy at school."

"Hasn't it always been that way?" I always expected things at school to suck, but Emily was more the sensitive, idealistic type. I think she expected stuff to get better, not worse.

"Not really," she said. "In the last year, it's gotten worse. The Internet stuff is just part of it. There's more drugs moving through the school than ever before, more kids stoned in class. More knives in lockers. And guns. I haven't seen any, but I hear some of the girls talk. I don't know how much is true, but if Mr. Miller or the principal knew the truth, they'd be freaking."

"Come on, it can't be that bad." Listen to me, Mr. Smiley Face.

"Colin, you sometimes have your head in the clouds. You must be able

27

to see how mean some people can be. It's been that way since elementary school, but now the nasty ones are selling drugs."

"You know, it's not worth getting worked up over a little weed."

"I'm not talking about weed. It's the other stuff. And it's getting ugly. Dealers trying to stake out territory. In the halls, even. And weapons in the lockers."

I'd heard rumors, but I guess I was just shutting most of it out. I still didn't want to believe her. "Why isn't somebody doing something to stop it?"

She gave me an icy look. "Because no one wants to get involved. No one wants to speak the truth or point a finger."

I sipped my coffee and watched her. She was visibly shaken. "Look at Liam and Craig, what they get away with, and that's just the tip of the iceberg," she said.

Just then I had an image in my head of a real iceberg. Big, white, magnificent.

And I wished Emily and I were somewhere on a sunny shoreline in the Arctic looking at that iceberg instead of here in a downtown coffee shop talking about how screwed up our world was.

"I'm worried about Amanda," she continued. "She's not returning my texts. I can't get her on her home phone. She's been away from school all week."

"Let's go talk to her," I said. I hated the feeling of sitting there doing nothing. If Amanda was hurting, we should go help her.

"Now?"

"Now," I said. I took Emily's hand as I stood up. She smiled. She seemed a little shocked at me touching her, but it was my way of trying to take charge. Something had to be done.

We walked through the cool dark night, and it felt good to be outside, even in this dingy part of the city. "I used to spend a lot of time walking around alone down here at night," I told Emily. "That was back when I was a smoker."

"You smoked cigarettes?" Emily seemed both surprised and appalled.

"Yeah. I used to smoke. How stupid is that? I have no excuses. Young and stupid, I guess."

"How'd you stop?"

"Cold turkey. That, and avoiding all smokers. When I used to walk around, I'd run into other kids smoking, and I'd stop and bum a cigarette or offer one to somebody I met. All very social. We'd stand around on the street and talk about one of two things. We always talked about smoking or how screwed up the world was. Sometimes both."

"Sounds like tons of fun."

I shrugged. "Sort of. But bad habits die hard."

"But you did it."

"One night I stayed home and read first-person accounts of lung cancer from smoking—hundreds of them on the Internet—for three straight hours. Then I looked in the mirror. Then I flushed my last pack—one at a time."

Em gave me one of her funny vegan looks. "Not very enviro-friendly. Kind of a waste of water." She was messing with me.

"It was a ritual. A necessary one. I promise to make it up to the environment."

Amanda's house looked dark except for one light on the second floor. There was no car in the driveway. Emily sent her a text telling her we were here. There was no response. So she called Amanda's cell phone. Once. Twice. Three times. On the fourth time, she answered.

"We need to talk," Emily insisted. "Colin is with me."

I could hear Amanda protesting, saying she was sleeping and telling us to leave.

"No," Emily insisted. "Let us in."

Amanda said something and then hung up.

"What," I asked.

"She said the door is unlocked. Let's go. I don't like the way she sounded."

So we walked in, turned a light on and found our way upstairs. I felt a little like a thief, a home invader. Her parents must have been out. Emily knew her way to Amanda's bedroom. When we opened the door, Amanda was sitting up in bed. At first I thought she was just really sleepy, but then I smelled the booze. Amanda was drunk.

"Amanda," Emily said, "what's going on? How come you haven't been in school?"

"I've been sick," she said.

"Bullshit," Emily said. "Colin talked to Liam. He's the one who posted those pictures. We can't let him get away with it."

"Forget it," Amanda said. "It's hope-less. They're out there now. You wouldn't believe the creepy emails I'm getting from guys."

"He did the same thing to me," I said. "I'm getting creepy emails from guys too. I just ignore them."

"But that's different for you. You're not me."

"But you have to do something," Emily said. "You can't just hole up in your room and get drunk."

"Why not?" Amanda asked. She sounded defeated. Hopeless.

"It was Liam, right?" I asked.

"Yeah. Craig is in on it too, I think."

"Of course," I said. "I don't think you were the first victim."

"Or the last," Emily added. "You need to blow the whistle on them. You need to make a stand."

"Not me, "Amanda said angrily. "I'm not like that." And then she lay back down in bed and pulled the covers over her head.

Emily and I just looked at each other. After about ten minutes, Amanda was asleep. She seemed okay, and we knew we should leave before her parents got home and started asking us questions.

As I walked Emily back to her house, I really craved a smoke. I hadn't felt that way in a long time. After I said goodbye to Emily, I walked back toward downtown on my own way home. Outside the Brown Bean, some kids from school were smoking. I bummed a cigarette from one of the girls, and she lit it, then smiled at me—kind of cute, kind of like we had this immediate bond because of the damn cigarette. I thought, maybe I should stay there and get to know her. But I felt the nicotine kick in, and I knew I needed to walk. I said thanks and walked on.

I smoked the cigarette down to the filter and even then took one last long draw. Then flicked it into the street the way I used to. I felt good. I felt stronger. But as I walked on, it occurred to me that I was losing ground.

Chapter Five

Part of me wanted to come up with a sneaky way to get back at Liam and Craig. Maybe do the same thing to them that they were doing to me and Emily's friends. I kept thinking maybe Emily would be next. If so, I'd slam those suckers somehow. As I walked to school the next morning, I called Emily and told her what I was thinking.

"Colin, it's so not you," she said. "It's not your style. Besides, I think it will backfire."

"But we need to do something—at least for Amanda and Marissa."

"Go to Mr. Miller. Tell him what's going on."

"Are you kidding?" I asked. "He already thinks I'm the troublemaker. And he thinks I'm a liar as well. Why don't you go talk to him?"

Emily was silent. She didn't have to say it. If she got involved, everyone would know one way or the other. That's the way it worked at school. And then if it wasn't Lump and Cave getting revenge, it would be someone else on her case for ratting.

"Damn," I said. "Miller hates my guts. I hate his guts. He'll think I've made up the whole thing and throw it back in my face. Who knows what will happen?"

"Colin?" I heard the pleading in her voice.

"Yeah?"

"If you don't speak up, no one will. Please?" The pleading again.

I sighed and wished I had another cigarette. Then I wished I hadn't smoked the one the night before. I also wished I wasn't going to school at all today and that I was asleep back home in bed. Then I sucked it up and said, "Yeah, I'll talk to Miller. But it's not going to be pretty." So right before class started, I politely asked my French teacher, Mademoiselle Leblanc, if I could go down to the office. A handful of kids coming into the classroom heard me. Word would be out. Damn.

I shuffled out of the classroom and hurried down the hall. The secretary asked me if Mr. Miller had called for me. I said no. She said he was busy.

I said it was important. She talked to him on the phone. A door opened.

"Colin? What brings you here?" he asked.

"We need to talk."

He gave me a puzzled look. The look also said he didn't trust whatever I was up to. He waved me into his office, and I slumped down into the hard wooden chair in front of his desk as he straightened his tie and returned to his throne. He didn't say anything but spread his hands and waited for me to speak.

I explained about the photo of me first.

"I'd gotten wind of it. But the word was you posted that photo yourself. Just trying to get attention. Not a particularly brilliant thing to do, but if it was done outside school, and it was, we decided we wouldn't touch it."

"But it wasn't me. That's not my body. Just my face. If you want me to prove it, I'll take my clothes off right here." Leave it to me to push all the wrong buttons.

Miller gave me a look of disgust. "Spare me, please. But, for the sake of argument, who is it you think is behind this prank?"

"Liam's the mastermind. Craig is along for the ride, I think."

"Same two boys you claimed were harassing the old man?"

"Yes."

"You have some kind of grudge match going on with each other?" he asked.

"No."

"Can't you just keep it outside the school grounds?"

That's when I explained about Amanda. "And she's not the only girl being harassed," I added.

"What would motivate anyone to do that?" he asked, still skeptical.

"It's like blackmail. A way to get some girl to do what they want."

Miller looked even more disgusted. "Like sexual favors?"

"Something like that," I said.

Miller looked doubtful. I could tell that he just wanted me to go away. And I knew he still didn't believe I was telling the truth. "So if this is really the case, Amanda should go to the police."

"She'd never do that."

"Then you should go to the police."

What a cop-out. "Right," I said. "Then have half the student body hate me."

"Hey, you've already ratted to me on your friends."

"They're not my friends," I said flatly. "And they deserve to be ratted out, but I came here hoping you might help me. And you're not willing to do that, are you?"

Miller was closing down. This meeting was coming to an end. "I don't know what else I can say," he concluded, which led me to understand that he didn't truly believe that this thing was playing out the way I described it.

I got up to go.

When my hand was on the door-knob, Mr. Miller suddenly added, "I'm going to ask around, see what I can find out about this sort of thing."

There wasn't any conviction in his voice. I figured it was just a brush-off so he could get on with his paperwork.

When I got back to class and found my seat, everyone was looking at me as if they knew where I'd been and what I was up to.

Chapter Six

Back in the hall, I had that craving again for a smoke. I was going to have to bust that one. No way was I going to go back to smoking. But it was an indicator that I was weak. That this was getting to me. Other kids were looking at me. A hint of a smile here and there. They probably liked the idea that maybe I was in trouble again. Maybe I was just paranoid. I wished that

I was older—out of school and away from here. I wished I was on a pilgrimage, hiking through the Himalayas. I blinked and waited for it to come true. But nothing changed. Same old school, same old halls, same old me.

And the same old rules.

I guess I wasn't paying much attention to where I was going. Someone opened a locker right in front of me. I smacked into it.

"Whoa, sorry, man," a voice said as I took a step back. It was Jerome. He was new this year. Word had it that he'd been transferred because of some kind of trouble at his other school.

I laughed. "No. My fault. Head in the clouds."

He smiled a kind of crooked smile. "It's cool. You're Colin, right?"

"Yep." I shrugged and started to walk away.

"Chill," Jerome said. "Wait till the crowd thins so we can talk." Jerome was one of those white-kid gangsta wannabes that I never understood. He had the look down and the body language, but it just didn't all come together as anything but a pose. But I was curious, so I hung back and waited for the crowds to thin.

"Too bad about that photo thing of you on the Internet. Dirty trick, whoever did it. Hey, I know what it feels like when people make fun of me. You know what I'm saying?"

I nodded. I'd always steered clear of Jerome because of his attitude, but here he was trying to show me a little concern. Weird.

"I always found ways to get back," Jerome said. "Check this out." From inside his locker, he took out a leather case of some sort, looked over his shoulder once, then opened it. Inside was a deadly-looking knife and a set of brass knuckles. "We all need to have some kind of self-defense these days, don't you think? And some way to get back at whoever is dogging you... if you have to."

Jerome closed the case and put it behind some textbooks in his locker. "If you're interested, I can set you up with whatever tools you might be needing. It'll cost you, but not that much."

I felt a little freaked at this. I'd seen Jerome himself hassling some younger kids at school. He was no saint. But was this part of his mission? Selling weapons on school property? Maybe Emily was right. Things were getting pretty nasty. Maybe I didn't have a clue. How had it come to this? "No thanks," I said. "Not my style."

Jerome gave me that crooked smile, and I couldn't quite guess what it meant.

"Just trying to help a brother out," he said, closing his locker. "Later." And he snapped the lock in place and walked off.

I sat with Emily in the cafeteria and told her about my meeting with Miller. I didn't say anything about Jerome. Emily seemed to be kind of moody. Maybe she was worried about Amanda and Marissa. Maybe she had other worries. Or it could have been me. In my head, I was still hiking the Himalayas, trying to make the whole school thing vanish.

Just then, a fight broke out. I'd noticed these two guys, Matthew and Tyler, arguing when I walked into the caf. Tyler was no saint, but Matthew was much worse. I'd known them both since elementary school. Matthew had been pushing little Tyler around plenty of times, but now Tyler was beginning to kick back. It was obvious from where I was watching that Matthew was the one who started this and the first one to throw a punch. Tyler just weaved out of the way for the first swipe. And the second. But Matthew landed a third on Tyler. Tyler went down but came up swinging.

Everyone else had already backed off and given them room to fight. People were shouting and cheering. No one moved to break it up. Miss Leblanc was the first teacher on the scene, and she bravely pushed through the mob and made a good effort to get them to stop. Matthew had Tyler down on the floor, using his advantage of weight and brute force. I couldn't see what was happening to poor Tyler, but, happily, I saw him pop back up onto his feet. Maybe he'd been taking self-defense classes or something. He got one good punch into Matthew's jaw just as Mr. Miller walked into the room and the crowd opened like the Red Sea to let him through. Everyone knew better than to get in Miller's way.

For an average-sized man, Miller seemed to have some incredible strength. He grabbed them both by the back of the shirt and pulled them apart. Within seconds, the two school security guards were on the scene and each took hold of one of the fighters. They walked them quickly out of the cafeteria, and the kids began to shuffle back to their seats.

"Wait," Mr. Miller shouted to them. The mob turned. Some were smirking. Some looked kind of sheepish. "Would someone tell me who started this?" He wasn't quite able to cover up how angry he was.

No one spoke a word. It would have been pretty obvious what the story was. But no one wanted to get involved. No one wanted to snitch. The old code of silence.

Mr. Miller looked angrier than ever. "Anyone?" he hollered.

Dead silence.

I wanted to stand up and tell Miller what he wanted to hear. But Emily touched my wrist and just shook her head. I glared at her, but I could see that she was concerned about me. I already had my issues. And I wasn't sure Miller would even want to hear from me again, not even on this. So I sat there and kept my mouth shut.

The cafeteria went strangely quiet then.

I felt a little nauseous and a bit disgusted as to how things had changed at school. Weapons, fights. No one speaking up about anything. Maybe those nights in the Himalayas would be pretty cold, but I couldn't help but think about being someplace far, far away from here.

Chapter Seven

The Himalayas were too far away,
so when I got home that night I retreated
to my sketchbook in my bedroom.
Ever since I was a little kid, I'd been
drawing things. I almost never showed
anyone my sketches. I'd always sketch
real things, usually animals, but put my
own interpretation on them.

I more or less raised myself. So being alone with a sketchbook was my idea of…well, not exactly being alone, if you know what I mean. I had my characters, my friends—snakes, dinosaurs, dogs, wizards, crazy caricatures of my teachers. The people all had big noses or big chins or big guts and, of course, women with big breasts. My creatures and humans all had big eyes—sort of Manga style.

My parents both had demanding jobs—ten to twelve hours a day. They always made sure there was food in the house and that all the bills were paid, but by the time they came home, they were beat and didn't have much time for me. They felt guilty about this, I know. But what the heck. It could have been a lot worse. Sometimes, when they were feeling like they'd truly ignored their kid, they'd buy me a new bike or something. At Christmas, I always made out big-time. Pretty much whatever I wanted. Truth is, I didn't want that much.

So there I was, alone in my room again, drawing in one of my dozens of sketchbooks, and I found myself sketching this amazing, ferocious rat.

As in ratting. Wasn't that the word that even Mr. Miller had used to describe me?

I created one rat and then another. Each more outrageous than the last. Until I hit on the one that seemed to just leap off the page. Big teeth, powerful body, large fierce eyes. But in those eyes was intelligence. The more I sketched in the details, the more he seemed to come alive. The more he seemed to mean something.

I was wondering why rats had such a bad rep. I wondered if they deserved it. I set the sketchbook upright on my desk and stared into those wild, dark, intelligent eyes.

It didn't take long to google the info I was looking for.

Rats. Highly intelligent rodents. The have strong teeth and can chew through concrete, cinder blocks, glass and aluminum. If they can't chew through something, they can squeeze themselves through a hole the size of a quarter. They can live pretty well anywhere on Earth because they are extremely adaptable and make good pets. They don't live very long though. Usually just a year or a year and a half. An adult female rat can have thirty-five baby rats a year. This apparently is because rats have a lot of sex. Up to twenty times a day. No lie.

They sleep a lot. Up to twenty hours a day. But when they are awake, they are very busy. One website argued that we unfairly label rats as dirty and dangerous and that we should learn to be kind to all rats. Sure, they were involved in killing half of Europe with the bubonic plague and other diseases, but it can be argued it was the fleas on the rats, not the rats themselves. And, like it or not, wherever there are humans, there are rats. So let's just figure out a way to cohabit with our hairy, horny, ambitious rats.

Above all, I kept reading that rats are survivors. Floods, earthquakes, volcanoes, war, even nuclear bombs. The rats survived. And, apparently, we have underestimated how smart rats really are.

I looked back at my masterpiece rat admiringly. It was only nine o'clock, and I was feeling fidgety. Oh, yeah, craving for a smoke. Big-time.

I stared straight into the eyes of my Manga-like rat. "Don't do it, dude," he seemed to be saying. "Stay focused."

Right.

So I took out a simple white T-shirt, the kind that my mom likes to buy me. I opened a drawer of my desk and took out the set of one hundred colored permanent markers she had given me for Christmas. I looked at my T-shirt, and I looked at my rat. "Do it, dude," he seemed to say.

Chapter Eight

I started wearing my rat T-shirt to school. I wore it under my shirt so no one actually saw it. I don't know why, but I felt better when I had it on. Stronger. So I made a few more. Different characters, different rats. All with the large intelligent eyes and big sharp teeth. All variations of rats. All variations of me, I told myself.

I thought things were cooling down at school. It was back to being dull routine as far as I could tell. So, like a good rat, I just stayed low to the ground and tried not to be noticed.

But then Emily told me that Amanda had transferred to another school. Marissa was thinking of doing the same. "They're both a mess," Emily said. "It wasn't just the photos. It's what people wrote as comments about them. A whole lot of lies posted by creeps who can remain anonymous. There's a hell of a lot of people out there who just want to hurt. And it's not just a few creepy guys. I don't get it."

Emily looked really concerned, really worried, but I had a feeling there was more to this.

"This stuff will just follow them both to wherever they go."

"I know. And once it's out there, it just gets reposted all over the place."

Now she looked even more worried.

"What?" I asked.

"Nothing."

"Bullshit."

She looked at me and then down at the floor. "Craig's doing it to me now," she said in a weak little voice that was not her style at all.

"Doing what exactly?"

"Asking for 'special favors' or he and Liam will give me the same treatment."

I was furious. I had lost my focus, been drifting along thinking things would improve, believing the problems would fade and go away. "They can't do that," I said.

"You've seen what they already got away with," she said. "And they'll get away with this too." And then, more sheepishly, she added, "But maybe I can talk them out of it."

"Yeah," I said, getting even more steamed. "If you agree to whatever those assholes want you to do."

She didn't say anything, and it suddenly began to dawn on me just how scared she was. Possibly even willing to go along with them in order to make it stop.

I shook my head. "No way, Emily. You're my friend. We've known each other for a long time. Let's stick it to them. Go with me to Miller's office. If he plays dumb again, let's go to the cops."

She had her head down again. "I can't do it, Colin."

"Why?"

"Because that would be ratting."

"So?" I was getting really pissed.

"You know what will happen. Liam and Craig will find a way to use that against me. To get people to turn against me. We've both seen this before."

"Your friends won't turn against you. Your real friends will support you."

She shook her head. "I can't," she said.

I had to keep my mouth shut just then. If I said the wrong thing (and I was the king of saying the wrong thing), she'd shut me down. Shut me off. I've had a long, unhappy career of speaking my mind, speaking the truth, to people who I considered friends only to have them shut me down for good.

"Emily," I said, in a low, controlled voice, "somebody has to do something. The code of silence is the code of bullshit."

She nodded. Her head was still down, and she couldn't look at me. She was sniffling, and I think a couple of tears fell from her eyes. "I'll be okay," she said. "Just don't do anything right now, please. Let me handle this."

Chapter Nine

Emily worked hard at avoiding me after that. She didn't answer my calls or my texts. I knew that if I went back to Miller's office to talk to him, she'd feel betrayed. I knew it was time to think outside the box.

Jerome was playing it up like he was my new best friend and still asking if I needed any help or any "tools," as he called it. But I just smiled and told him everything was cool. I didn't want anything to do with whatever business he had going on. But then he caught me off guard as I was walking home from school through the park. He caught up with me and said he'd had "some good luck," that he'd scored some great weed. He offered me a little Baggie with several joints. "I got lots," he said. "This one's on the house."

I was tempted, but I turned him down. I knew it might make things go away for a while, but I also knew that those things would still be there later. I was worried about Emily. And I felt that I hadn't solved the dilemma of Liam and Craig. It looked like they could just float through life wreaking whatever damage they wanted and not be held accountable. What would they be like once they left the lowly confines of high school and moved out into the big world?

By the time I got home, I knew what I needed to do.

Not being the most social animal (unlike the rat on my T-shirt), it took a dozen or so emails to kids I knew to gather even more email addresses until I had at least a hundred contacts from school. Some were kids I knew well, others were a bit more distant. But all were people I thought would be "sensitive" to the issue at hand.

I didn't mention Emily. And I didn't even mention Amanda and Marissa by name, but I did spill the beans on exactly what Craig and Liam were doing to girls at school. It was a straightforward statement of fact. And I signed my name to it. I even put a little signature image of one of my Manga rats by my name. An anonymous email would not work. And I asked all one hundred or so to pass it on.

I hesitated and then pressed *Send*. I guess I could have sent a group email, but I wanted to send them one by one so everyone would understand it was a personal message from me.

Colin. The snitch. The whistle-blower. The stool pigeon. The tattletale. The informer. The rat.

I was still at the keyboard sending out the news when messages started to come back at me. There were a couple of good ones cheering me on. But there were some really nasty ones telling me to mind my own business—in much less polite terms.

Around eleven that night, I even got a phone call from Emily, even though she hadn't even been on my mail-out list. Somebody had forwarded my email to her. "Colin, you've got to send another email saying you were lying. Tell them it was a hoax. Do it now."

"I can't do that."

"You have to."

"I think it's too late," I said. "What's done is done."

Emily sounded exasperated. "The girl who emailed this to me—I think she was targeted by Liam before. She's afraid her story will get out. They never posted any pictures, but they threatened to."

"And that probably means they got her to do what they wanted."

"Maybe. But now she's afraid everyone will know if the full story gets out about Liam and Craig."

"I feel bad for her," I said defiantly, "but these guys need a wake-up call. Tonight was the night."

"Colin, sometimes you are so pigheaded," she said angrily.

"Sorry" was all I could bring myself to say, and she hung up.

As I sat there in the silence of my room, I suddenly wondered if I had been irrational and stupid. It wouldn't have been the first time I acted out what I was certain was the right thing to do, only to have it come back and bite me in my ass. I wondered if Emily would write me off for good now. Even though I was trying to help her, Amanda and Marissa— and whoever else had been victimized.

And, at that point, I grew really tired. The fight was all out of me. I turned off my computer so I couldn't read any more incoming mail. I turned off my cell phone too. I opened up a brand-new sketchbook and drew an eagle soaring high over some mountains.

Chapter Ten

The next morning, I was expecting to get nailed in one way or another by Liam and Craig. When I got to school, I sat down on the wall outside, seeing if they would spot me. I figured it beat the hell out of waiting for them to sneak up on me. As I sat there, I sketched in my little pocket drawing pad. For too long, I had stopped carrying it around, knowing other kids thought it was weird, but now I didn't care. I had my latest rat T-shirt on under my hoodie, and that felt good, even though it wouldn't help with what was coming.

Oddly enough, it was Jerome who was the first to say anything. "Good work, Colin. Nailed their balls to the wall."

Getting praise from Jerome should have clued me in that the shit was about to hit the fan, but I appreciated the support. "It was all I could think to do. Those guys were out of control."

"Understood. I appreciate what it took. But watch your back, bro. And remember, I'm around if you need support. Maybe we could clean this shithole up by weeding out some of the whackers and inbreds."

I nodded but could see that Jerome's idea of school improvement was a bit different from mine.

Kids were pouring into the school now. Most were just ignoring me as usual.

But as I scanned the faces, I recognized some of my classmates who had received my little newsflash. I got a couple of thumbs-up but a lot more dirty looks. Emily and a couple of other girls walked on by. Emily didn't even look at me, but her friends, Rachel and Ashley, looked at me like I'd committed some crime against humanity. Kyle, a friend of Liam's, was the first one to come up to me and speak his mind, what little of it there was. "You freakin' stupid or what? You can't go ratting on your own. It's just not done." I could hear the threat in his voice.

"Just telling it the way it is. Just speaking the truth."

He put his face up close to me. I could see the weird glint of anger in his eyes. I didn't flinch. "No such thing as truth, man," he said. "It's all bullshit, and all we can do is hang together."

I didn't say anything. What was there to say? The crowd was thinning, but I was still watching the faces. Dirty looks. Not everyone. But enough. It was out now. Colin, the rat. Guess I'd have to wear that one until I graduated.

Liam and Craig were conveniently absent from school that day. I tried to savor the kind words from a handful of girls who talked to me through the day. These were friends of Amanda and Marissa. It was Stephanie who said, "That was brave, Colin. A little out there. But brave. Some of us get it. You stuck your neck out when no one else would."

"Thanks," I said, realizing this was the first time Stephanie had ever given me the time of day. Maybe this would turn out all right after all.

"Anyway, Marissa followed Amanda's lead. She's transferred too. So everything's good now."

I wanted to say that everything wasn't good, but I didn't. It looked like the rat had at least one admirer and that look she gave me was nothing short of sweet. She touched my sleeve as she walked away. Very sweet.

After a bit, I got used to all those looks—those silent opinions. Mostly negative. To hell with it. What's done is done. After third period, I went looking for Emily on her usual route from English to math.

"I don't want to talk about it," she said. "It was a dumb thing to do."

"No, it wasn't. It was the right thing to do."

"It doesn't matter now. Amanda and Marissa have transferred. So it's over."

"Yeah, but what about you?"

"I could have handled it."

"You're mad at me?"

Emily looked confused. "Not exactly mad. It's just that being seen with you makes people think I was part of it."

This really wasn't like the old Emily. The vegan student activist Emily.

She usually didn't care what opinions people had of her. This was different.

"Meet me at the Brown Bean after school, okay?" I said. "We need to talk."

She shook her head. "No. Let's let it all cool off for a bit." And she walked off clutching her textbooks to her chest.

I was left feeling abandoned. What the hell was this? My one good friend was more worried about what kids would think than about me.

Later in the day, when my path crossed Stephanie's again, she smiled so sweetly that I stopped to speak to her. She seemed a little nervous, probably because of the way other kids were watching us. "Could I buy you a coffee at the Brown Bean after classes?" I asked.

She looked surprised and a bit awkward. She didn't have to say it. The answer was no. Maybe she didn't want to be seen with the rat either.

"It's okay," I said. "Maybe another time.

She nodded and walked off. So much for my attempt at romance.

At home after school, I turned on my computer and looked up *rat* again, this time coming across "Year of the Rat." I discovered that, traditionally, the Chinese had great respect for rats, which were considered courageous, shrewd, ambitious, inventive and highly adaptable. A rat year is a time of renewal and hard work. It even turned out that I was born in the year of the fire rat. *Fire rats tend to be energetic decision makers. They are loners and are also known to have little self-control.* I could deny none of this Maybe the ancient Chinese knew what they were talking about. But then there was this: *Rats tend to make enemies and often lack the tact to diffuse them.*

I had to laugh out loud.

So I took out my last plain white T-shirt and took out my markers. I thumbed through my sketches until I found the drawing that fit what I had just learned about rats, and about me. I took my time, making this one the best and most outrageous one yet.

And when I finished it, I put on the shirt and looked at myself in the mirror. I decided then and there this one was too good to hide under my hoodie. This rat was ready to face the world.

Chapter Eleven

Wearing my rat T-shirt on the outside
definitely did the trick.

It caught everyone's attention, and
the response ranged from being laughed
at to being called a variety of insulting
names. I kept my head high and tried to
ignore it all, but on the second day of
wearing my rat shirt, Emily ran toward
me in the hall. I thought she was going

to hit me. She looked all worked up about something.

"Take it off, you idiot," she insisted.

"You don't like my art?"

"I like your art fine. You just don't need to draw more attention to yourself."

I was still feeling pretty defensive and hurt about how Emily had abandoned me.

"Look," she said. "Liam's mother was forwarded your email. So was Craig's father. It was bound to happen. They've been busted—by their parents at least. The photos of Marissa and Amanda are gone. And they're leaving me alone. You can back off now."

I smiled. "Cool. What about that photo of me?"

"It's still there. I checked."

I smiled some more. "Hell, I don't care. It means they still see me as a threat. And that's good."

"You don't feel violated by that photo being up?"

"Not really," I said. "It's not my body."

"But other people think it's you."

"I'm working pretty hard to avoid worrying about what other people think."

"What about the shirt?"

"Okay," I said and stripped it off, leaving me wearing my long-sleeved button-down shirt that I had on under it. "Now I look like any other guy at school."

"No," Emily said, suddenly allowing a smile. "You're way better-looking than those other guys."

I must have given her a puzzled look. She'd never actually flirted with me before. "Go for coffee after school?" I asked.

She nodded.

I guess the train was back on the rails. For now at least.

Mr. Miller called me down to the office later that day.

"Where's the shirt?" he blurted out.

"What shirt?" I asked.

"You know what I'm talking about."

I pulled it out of my backpack and handed it to him. He held it up to the light. His brow scrunched up as he studied it. "You make this?"

"Yeah."

"It's good. Weird but good. You should be studying art."

"It was dropped from the curriculum in last year's budget cuts, remember?"

"I'm just trying to say you have talent."

"Thank you."

"I was going to tell you not to wear this thing. Teachers say it is a disruptive influence."

"Really?" I said, feeling defensive.

Miller noted my sarcasm. He shook his head and rubbed his nose. He was smiling now. "Look, Colin. I know what you did for Amanda and Marissa. I didn't like doing it, but I approved their transfer from here. I couldn't seem to solve that problem within the workings of the system. But maybe you solved it for me."

"Are you congratulating me for that?"

"Off the record, yes. But I don't approve of vigilantism."

"Another big word. So why'd you call me here, exactly?"

Now Miller looked a bit more serious. "I know I should have done something about those two. Truth is, I think that was small potatoes compared to some other stuff going on at the school."

"Like what?"

"I can't say. You have any clues as to what I'm talking about?"

I was thinking of Jerome and his "tools." And I was thinking about what Emily had said before about how the climate of the high school had changed. "Not really," I answered.

"Well, maybe you could keep your ear to the ground for me, and we could have a little chat once in a while."

I looked hard at Miller, feeling a little pissed off. He wanted to use me. "You want me to be your mole? Your spy? Your snitch?"

Miller was serious now. He handed me back my T-shirt and pointed to the artwork on the front. Yeah, he wanted me to be a rat—his rat.

I took the shirt and stuffed it in my backpack. "No way," I said defiantly. "Not in a million years."

Chapter Twelve

It was a quiet week after that. I kept waiting for the ax to fall. Waiting for something to happen. Instead, it was just a dull old school week.

Until Friday afternoon rolled around.

Like everyone else, I heard the shots. Three of them. It was unmistakable. Someone was shooting in the hallway.

I was in history class at the time. Ms. Reitman stopped speaking and, as a couple of my classmates got out of their seats and started toward the door, she blocked them and then stood there with her arms folded. "No one leaves," she said. "No one. You know the drill."

I guess it was what they call a lockdown. After a few silent, tense minutes, we heard sirens and then saw four police cars pulling up in front of the school. Then we heard them in the halls. After about ten minutes, one of the cops tapped on the door and identified himself. Ms. Reitman opened the door. "Everything okay in here?" he said.

Ms. Reitman nodded, and he left.

When the bell rang to change classes, Ms. Reitman insisted we stay put.

Eventually, Mr. Miller came over the PA system. "I want to first thank you all for your cooperation," he said in an authoritative voice. "What you heard earlier were gunshots. Someone—we don't know who—came into the school and fired three shots. No one was hit. No one was hurt. The shooter then ran off. As of now, the school is safe. Police are here, and they've searched the building. In a few minutes, we'll be dismissing you to go home. Police will remain onsite until the building is empty.

"I'd appreciate your further cooperation on this. Leave the building calmly and in an orderly fashion when your teacher dismisses you. And finally, if anyone has any information about this incident, anything at all about why someone would be shooting in our school, please come forward and speak to me. Thank you."

We had to stay in our seats for twenty more minutes before it was our class's turn to leave. I was thinking about what Emily had said about things getting weirder and weirder at our school.

Weapons, drugs. The two somehow tied together. It made my little problems with Liam and Craig seem pretty minor. But I couldn't help thinking about Jerome. Maybe he was at the center of this. And I remembered that he tried to give me some weed. Didn't he say he had other stuff? Harder, more dangerous drugs, for sure.

We weren't allowed to go to our lockers. As I walked out the front door of the school, it felt truly bizarre, like something out of a TV cop show. We walked past armed policemen lined up on either side. And there must have been at least twelve police cars on the street. Whatever had gone down, they were taking this very, very seriously.

As I walked on, I heard someone coming up behind me. And then there was a hand holding mine. Emily.

"I'm scared," she said, squeezing my hand.

"I know," I said. "I'll walk you home."

"Thanks."

We walked in silence until we were downtown. Once we were away from the school, the whole thing that had happened seemed completely unreal.

"Did anyone see what happened?" I asked.

"I don't think so. But word is, someone came into the school and tried to shoot one of the students. He must have been pretty brave to do it in the middle of the day."

"Or pretty crazy. Was it a real gun or a pellet gun?" I asked.

"I saw the police looking at a couple of bullets that were dropped. They looked real to me. And it sounded like a real gun."

"Why would someone do this?" I wondered. "And why do you know so much about it?"

"Drugs. Money. Some kind of territorial thing. That's the gossip. And I know because I listen to gossip and I pay attention to what's going on."

"Who were they shooting at?"

"Jerome. He's been dealing. And he's new this year," said Emily. "He's selling on what used to be some other dealer's turf."

It started to make a bit of sense. And it was Jerome who had his own "tools" for self-defense. If he had knives, he probably also had guns. And so did his competition. "Damn. Do you think the shooter will be back?"

"I doubt it. Miller will have cops at the school every day now until they catch whoever did the shooting."

"Does anybody know who it is?"

"It wouldn't be hard to figure it out. Jerome could probably name him."

"But Jerome won't talk?"

"Of course not. If he did, he'd have to admit to what he's been doing."

"But someone needs to say something. At least let the cops know that it was Jerome they were trying to shoot."

Emily saw the look on my face. She squeezed my hand tighter now. "Don't get involved, Colin. Please, don't say a word."

Chapter Thirteen

I considered tracking Jerome down myself and convincing him to go to the police. What if the shooter did come back to the school? Someone could get killed. It might not matter if police were there or not. Whoever was after Jerome was angry and reckless. Armed and dangerous. For sure, Jerome knew who it was. He needed to talk.

But that wasn't going to happen. The story was on the TV news and in the newspapers. No one from school was offering up any clues. One report even suggested that several students had seen the guy shooting but no one would say a word. Same as always.

My parents were both home for dinner that night, a rare event for sure. They wanted to know all about what happened at school. I'd never seen them so concerned. My dad, who had never laid down any rules since I was thirteen, said, "I want you to stay home tonight. I'd rather you didn't go out."

"Sure," I said. I didn't go out that much anyway. Even on a Friday night.

I holed up in my room instead and returned to the fantasy world in my sketchbooks. I was moving on to creating fantastic winged creatures. And while I was drawing, I realized how easy it would be to go to a pay phone, make an anonymous call to the police and just let them know it was Jerome who was the intended victim. It would at least set them on the trail.

But I didn't do it.

Instead, I fell sound asleep.

I didn't hear the news until the next afternoon. Emily called my cell and blurted it out. "Jerome was shot dead. He was home. I just heard it on the news. The police aren't saying much more." Emily sounded upset. And scared.

I was shocked. "I almost called the police last night and told them about Jerome. If I had, this wouldn't have happened."

"You can't blame yourself for this," she said. "Jerome brought this on himself."

"But he didn't deserve to die," I said.

"Can you come over?" Emily asked.

I took a deep breath. "Not right now, Em. Sorry. I just need to be by myself."

I needed to get out of the house, though, before my parents heard the news and came home to lay down more rules. So I walked.

Somehow the streets, the houses, the trees all looked different. It wasn't like Jerome was some great guy. It wasn't like he was a close friend or even a friend at all. But he was just a kid like me, and he'd made a couple of wrong turns. And then this. Damn. Was it that easy to screw up and end up dead? I couldn't stop thinking that if I had said something—anything—to Mr. Miller, even, it would have set in motion a completely different chain of events. They might have opened Jerome's locker. The police would have questioned him. Maybe he'd even have been arrested.

But at least he'd be alive.

I walked down to the harbor and looked out over the water. It was calm and peaceful. But it wasn't enough. I should have done something. But I hadn't. As I walked home, I convinced myself that it was too late now to do anything. It was over. The deed was done.

At home, I was totally freaked to see a police car in front of my house. My parents' cars weren't there, so I figured they weren't home yet. I didn't look at the cop sitting in the car as I walked past him and up to my front door. As I was putting the key into the lock, I heard him get out of the car and walk my way.

"Are you Colin? Colin Reed?"

I turned slowly around. "Yes."

"Can I ask you some questions? I guess you heard about what happened to Jerome Jeffreys."

I nodded.

"Are your parents home?"

"No," I said.

"You want to wait until they get here?"

"No," I said. "Come on in."

We sat down at the kitchen table. "Listen," he said. "You aren't in trouble. This isn't about you. We're just trying to piece things together to find out who was out to get Jerome."

"But why ask me? I wasn't exactly close to him."

"I'm sure you weren't. All we know is that someone saw you with Jerome in Fielder Park last week. That's all. Someone gave us your name. So here I am."

"We were just talking."

"Fine. But can you give us anything to go on? Any reason why someone would try to kill Jerome."

I took a deep breath. "Jerome sold drugs," I said. "Weed and other stuff. I don't know what." I paused and looked at him. He didn't seem surprised.

"And he had weapons. Knives, pellet guns, I think. Maybe more. He was selling weapons to students, I think. Supposedly for self-defense."

"You buy any of those weapons from him? I hear you've had some of your own rough times at school."

He'd probably spoken to Miller. Maybe it was Miller who had steered him my way. Miller who believed I'd at least tell what I knew about Jerome.

"No," I said. "I never bought any weapons from him. He offered though."

"You buy anything else from him?"

"No," I said.

"Okay, so he had the drugs and weapons," he said. "But why was someone so intent on shooting him that they would waltz into your school in the middle of the day and blast away?"

"Jerome was new this year. I can't say this for a fact, but there was already someone in our school selling weed and stuff. Maybe more than one person. But when Jerome came to the school, he was tromping into someone else's territory."

"Do you know who that someone is?" he asked.

"No, I don't." I shrugged. "But I don't think it would be that hard to find out."

"That's the funny part, Colin. You'd think that'd be as plain as day. But it isn't. We ask a lot of questions and don't get many answers. Makes our job a whole lot harder. But, hey, thanks for speaking with me. Here's my card. If you can tell me anything else, let me know."

He got up from the table and headed for the door. I felt good about what I'd had to offer, even though it wasn't much. Before he left the kitchen, though, he turned. "Colin, I wasn't going to say this, but I have to get it off my chest. If you had gone to one of your teachers or come to us and told us what you did just now, my guess is that Jerome would not be dead. Sometimes silence kills."

I watched as he turned away and walked out the door.

Chapter Fourteen

School was canceled for two days as the police searched all the lockers. Once they'd found the weapons in Jerome's locker, Miller asked the cops to scour every square inch of the school. They found more, and it was all over the news. The city was shocked. Parents couldn't seem to understand how it had become so easy for teenagers to get their hands on not just knives, pepper spray and pellet guns, but real guns as well. It was even harder for them to imagine why so many kids, even the good kids, felt they needed these weapons in or out of school.

When we returned to classes that Wednesday, police watched us as we entered the building. They'd also installed two metal detectors we had to walk through as we entered. It was like getting on an airplane. Everything about school now seemed charged with a nervous fear.

Emily wasn't in class, and she wasn't replying to my emails or calls. I went to her house, but her mother wouldn't let me see her. She somehow knew that the police had come to my house. A lot of people knew. Someone in my neighborhood had spread that one. And so people thought I might be involved in whatever Jerome had been doing. But while I was standing there getting the cold shoulder from Emily's mother, Emily came to the door. When she hugged me, her mother backed off and left us alone. Emily led me inside. We sat down in the living room. "I don't think I can go back," she said. "It's not just Jerome. You've heard the news. You know what they found. How could that be our school? My parents are thinking of letting me sit out the rest of the year and maybe go to private school to finish my last two years."

"Emily, come on. Come back. I miss you." I meant it. With all the crap happening around me, I felt more alone than ever. I had always told myself that I didn't need anyone, that I was good on my own. But I felt different now. Emily was one of the few people on the planet that I felt understood me. Maybe the only person at school I felt truly connected to. And maybe my feelings were stronger than that. I think I had been covering up what I really felt about her. I knew that now.

I think she was shocked to hear me say I missed her. She smiled the sweetest smile I'd ever seen. "Really?"

"Really," I said. "Come back. I'll be there for you."

"Not yet," she said.

"But you'll talk to me on the phone, right?"

"Sure. I'm sorry. I shouldn't have been ignoring you."

"That's okay. It's been a confusing time," I said. "For all of us."

Two weeks went by, and Jerome's killer had still not been found. Police said they had leads, but that was all. Everyone at school was paranoid. Teachers were really shaken. When any little confrontation occurred, the ever-present hallway cops were right on it. I think, for me, the most unnerving part was that the cops wore bulletproof vests. It was as if they were expecting Jerome's killer, or someone equally violent, to show up any day.

Attendance was way down. Many parents were keeping their kids home. My mother suggested that to me. But I said no way. It was a funny thing. I'd never really liked school. I disliked the social games, found many of my classes boring and couldn't wait for my high school sentence to be over. But it was different now. I wasn't going to let this thing with Jerome, and the fear it created, stop me from getting an education. I know how lame that sounds, but in some strange way it was true.

Jerome's killer finally turned himself in three weeks after the murder. His name was James Gleason. He was nineteen and not in school. He'd been in lots of trouble before, and he'd been dealing drugs on the street and outside our school. And then Jerome moved into his territory. Gleason was charged with first-degree murder. It was all anyone wanted to talk about in school.

But here's the thing. Gleason turned himself in. No one had come forward to suggest he might have been the shooter in the school that day, and it was obvious that some students had seen him in the hall. Someone would have known who he was. Even after Jerome was shot, no one spoke up about this dangerous guy who obviously wanted to wipe out the competition. Now everybody just kept saying how happy they were that he was caught and this whole thing was over.

In my head, it wasn't over. I kept thinking that if we weren't watching out for each other, even the Jeromes of the world, then something like this would just happen again. But I kept it to myself. I especially didn't say it to Emily. She had returned to school right after

Gleason's confession. She, like everyone, was breathing a sigh of relief. But not me. The police were now absent from the hallways, but no one was planning on removing the metal detectors.

Chapter Fifteen

I kept mostly to myself except for the time I spent with Emily. She was back in school now and things there had settled down quite a bit. I wasn't the only one wishing this school year was over and this was all behind us. But I kept my head down and made a point of not getting involved in anyone's business.

That was until it became painfully obvious to me that someone had decided to pick up where Gleason and Jerome had left off. There was a vacuum to be filled. Jacob was a friend of Liam and Craig's. (Surprise, surprise.) He'd dropped out of school awhile back, missed a year, but then dropped back in, so he was older than most kids in our class. Emily told me that she heard he was selling weed.

But there was more to it than that. I heard he was also selling crystal meth and crack. Some kids said he'd been dealing on the street while he was out of school, that he'd been working with whoever had been supplying Jerome. Others said he'd been with Gleason's supplier.

I wasn't gullible enough to believe everything people said, but I kept an eye on Jacob, and I could see that he had his own little posse of wannabes, including Liam and Craig, who trekked off with him after school. It wasn't too difficult to watch a couple of deals go down.

"What if I just confront him?" I asked Emily. "Just tell him flat-out that he's got to quit or I'll snitch."

Emily looked frightened. "You can't do that. It doesn't work that way. You'll get hurt."

"But this is the loop. What if it plays out the same way again? Besides, I'm hearing stories about some kids getting pretty wasted and downright sick on some of the meth he's dealing. It's all bad news as far as I can see."

"Can't you just leave it alone?"

"No," I said. "I can't. That's what I did before."

I thought Emily was going to get mad at me. She looked scared. "Tell Miller. Just tell him what you know and walk away from it."

She was right. I would have preferred the confrontation with Jacob.

I really would. But I'd settle for this. Cowardly, but better than nothing. Miller would listen to me this time.

I waited until school was over. I told Emily to head home and not wait for me. When the halls were empty, I knocked on Mr. Miller's door.

"It's open."

I walked in. He seemed surprised to see me. "Colin, come in."

I told him what I knew. Or thought I knew. "Look," I said, "I know Jacob's involved in something. Like Jerome was. I don't know the whole story, and I don't believe half of what other kids say, but the rat in me says I need to do this."

Miller looked puzzled. "How come we don't know more about this?"

"'Cause what's going down is mostly off school grounds. But he's here every day and making contacts. It's a problem that won't go away."

Mr. Miller ran his hand across his forehead. "I can't afford to ignore what you're telling me."

"No, you can't."

"If we go after Jacob, is he going to know that it was you who put us on his trail?"

"Probably. That's my rep. And if he can't figure it out, I'm sure Liam will give him a good hint."

"Is that what this is about? You still trying to get even with Liam and Craig?"

"No way," I said, feeling ticked off at Miller again. It was like he still didn't trust me.

He nodded. "Okay, I'll follow up on this. We're pretty tight with the police these days, as you might expect. We'll see what they have to say about Jacob. But, Colin, I have to ask you something."

"What?"

"Back before Jerome got shot, someone saw you with him in the park.

It was just a person living near there. Someone had made an anonymous phone call to the police saying you were seen buying drugs from Jerome. Is that true?"

My eyes went a little blurry then. It totally caught me off guard. But if I wanted him to believe me, I knew I couldn't bullshit him. He'd see right through it. "No," I said. "He offered me some, but I didn't take it."

What he said next shocked me. "Thanks for being honest with me, Colin. And thanks for coming by."

Chapter Sixteen

Mr. Miller wasn't quite as discreet as I thought he'd be when it came to looking into Jacob's activities. When the time came for the police to question him at school, he was clean. Not only had he stopped dealing (at least temporarily), but his teachers had nothing bad to say about him or his work. He had cleaned up his act.

But Liam had probably told him that I was the one who had ratted on him. I knew this because a pair of new Photoshopped images of me appeared on GoofFace. Not the real me, of course. And these were pretty disgusting. I didn't think that was all there was to it though. I knew there'd be more than that.

But I wasn't expecting what happened next.

I met Emily outside school one morning a few days after Jacob was questioned by the police.

"It's Amanda," she said. "More of those pictures surfaced on the Internet. She tried to kill herself with pills and booze. She's in the hospital."

"Is she going to be okay?"

"I think so," Emily said. "But why is this happening?"

"It's Liam trying to get back at me for squealing on Jacob."

"I can't believe she tried to kill herself," Emily said.

"Maybe the pictures are their way of trying to get to me," I said. "I'm sorry. I didn't think they'd go back to such sick stuff. They haven't tried to get to you?"

"No photos," she said. "But I've had a couple of emails."

"I'm sorry. Maybe you shouldn't be hanging out with me."

"Colin, you're the best thing that ever happened to me. But I'm scared."

"I'm going to bypass Miller and go to the cops. I can at least file a complaint about what they're doing to me. I'll tell them about Amanda and let them look into it."

"If you do that, everyone will know."

"I don't care," I said angrily.

"I'll go with you," Emily said.

But I wouldn't let her do that. I needed to do this on my own.

I had to stop them before they got to Amanda again. And before they got to Marissa. Or to Emily.

It wasn't long before everyone at school knew about my visit to the police. Liam and Craig were questioned but not charged. The pictures of Amanda came down but not mine. I started getting emails from wackos. Worse than that were the nasty emails from other kids. Mostly anonymous. Mostly angry that I would rat on Liam and Craig.

Emily and I honed our Internet skills and figured out how to delete just about any photo or any posting from any site. I guess you might call it hacking. We could have put up pictures of Liam or Craig if we wanted to. We could have made them appear in whatever ridiculous situation we wanted. But we didn't. And I left those pictures of me out there. Just to prove I didn't care.

Amanda was getting counseling. She was even talking about coming back to school. She said she didn't like her new school.

When the heat was off, Jacob must have gone back to his trade.

And got busted.

That wasn't my doing, but I was blamed for it.

I think I must have attracted quite a following of people who had opinions about me who didn't even know me. I started wearing my rat shirt to school again. I had created four of them, each more outrageous than the last. I remembered what was said about someone born in the year of the rat: *quick-witted, intelligent; can react swiftly to his environment; someone who is highly adaptive. A survivor.*

Graffiti was starting to appear on the walls of the school. *Colin the Rat* was scrawled, usually alongside a very insulting image. It was just chalk at first. But then spray paint.

Liam and Craig finally caught up with me one night when I was walking home from Emily's by myself. They'd been drinking. Maybe doing something else too. Jacob was with them.

"Hey, Pretty Boy," Liam said, putting himself directly in front of me.

"Hey," I said, trying to stay cool.

I wasn't much of a fighter, never was, never will be. I knew I wouldn't stand a chance against the three of them.

I don't know why, but I wasn't scared. I decided to speak my mind to all three and tell them what I thought. I even owned up to going to the police. But they already knew that. After my little speech, I still stood my ground. I should have done what an honest rat would have done. I should have run. But I didn't.

That's when they beat the crap out of me. Craig held my arms. Liam and Jacob took turns. I kept waiting for a knife blade.

But they were kind.

They left me punched up good, bruised and bleeding from the lip and over the eye. I was lying there on the sidewalk until some man out walking his dog came by.

My parents wanted me to go to the police, but I'd done enough of that. I convinced them I was okay.

Instead, the next day I put on my most outrageous rat shirt, and I went back to school. I felt terrible. I was sore and aching. And I looked like shit. I looked exactly like I felt. But I didn't have to explain to anyone what had happened. Anyone who cared already knew. One of the daring threesome had bragged about it. And word spread.

During school, I started getting some text messages with variations of *You got what you deserved.* Idiots. Aside from when we were in class, Emily didn't let me out of her sight. She was there at the door of every one of my classes when the bell rang. She walked me through the halls.

Mr. Miller stopped me as we passed him, gave me a very concerned look and said, "Do you want to talk?"

"No," I said. "Nothing to talk about."

I'd talk to him again when I had some important information. Once a rat, always a rat. But this was different.

So the wounds healed nicely, the bruises faded and school got strangely... well, dull again. All except for the fact that Liam and Craig picked on the wrong girl as their next victim. Lauren's father was a lawyer, and he went straight to the cops. He had the evidence and the means, and he nailed them.

But the graffiti was on the increase. On the school walls outside and on some old buildings and construction sites downtown. It used to be just a hasty scrawl with a cheap can of spray paint—*Colin the Rat*, with a crude ugly rodent with an ugly face.

But now it was different. The artwork was better. Much better. It was multicolored, and the script was elegant. The rat in the graffiti was more than a little Manga. The rat sometimes looked a lot like the rat on my T-shirts, the rat that I came up with.

Mr. Miller and the principal were so pissed off about having to sandblast the brick walls that they called me in for a consultation as to how to get the graffiti to stop. Miller even caught on that the artwork was good. "This isn't just vandalism anymore, Colin. This is serious, premeditated art." He paused. "But it's still a nuisance. And it's costing the school money."

Maybe he thought I'd rat on whoever it was. But I couldn't.

I started to see variations of the rat image all over town. There were even stenciled versions on sidewalks. There was an article about it in the weekly newspaper, *The Coast*.

It had become clear to me that Colin the Rat had at least as many anonymous admirers as he had detractors.

Emily said, "I think you somehow raised ratting to a whole new level of social acceptance."

And I guess I could take that as a compliment.

Long live the rat.

Lesley Choyce divides his time between teaching, writing, running Pottersfield Press and surfing the waves of the North Atlantic. He is the author of almost eighty books for youth and adults. Lesley lives in Lawrencetown Beach, Nova Scotia.